The Garden Flowers

A Tale of Growth, Faith, and Letting Go

Lawrence Quigley

BlueRose ONE .com
Stories Matter

BLUEROSE PUBLISHERS UK Ltd.
London

This book is primarily published and distributed in Great Britain and is also available in other global marketplaces.

ISBN: 978-93-7310-743-1

Designed and distributed by **BlueRoseONE.com** with global reach. Printing and fulfilment are managed through international distribution networks, ensuring availability based on order locations.

For publishing inquiries, visit **www.BlueRoseONE.com**

BlueRose Publishers UK Ltd,
Unit 3, 6-7 St Mary at Hill, London

+44 7386286323

First Edition: October 2025

Contents

1 | The Garden Flowers

Part 1:
The Beginning

A flower was picked and re-planted in another part of the garden. The flower was in strange soil there, and felt that he couldn't grow as well as he could in his own part of the garden. He was very sad at this.

The garden fence blocked out all of the sunshine, and only rarely would the rain trickle through the overhanging branches of the large Oak tree nearby. He was amongst different flowers to his own, and he felt very alone.

Soon, however, he found that the same bees were buzzing about in the air - the same ones that used to kiss his petals in the other part of the garden; and they did it again!... even bigger kisses this time. This cheered up the flower very much, and he laughed and laughed when the bees kissed him; and in time, he began to laugh with the other peculiar flowers, until eventually the flower laughed all the time.

Not long after, the garden fence was removed and the sun shone on him all day, bringing more bees to laugh with.

In time, he was re-planted again and again, and he was happy and looked forward to being re-planted.

Soon, however, the flower began to fade and wither; but the bees still

kissed his petals, until one day they kissed the last remaining petal left on the flower.

And this last petal blew in the wind, gently across the garden it wafted - and landed in the place from which it first grew. And it sank into the ground and was buried with the kisses of the bees on it......whereupon, another little flower immediately took root and began to grow. But this little flower had no need for the bees kisses, for its petals were filled with the laughter and joy from the petal from which it had grown - and the bees still buzzed in the air, and the little flower still felt their hidden kisses.

Now this particular little flower had seven petals, which in time began to die - as petals of all flowers must.

Each day, one of the petals would be carried on the wind and blown this way or that, finally coming to rest near or far away from whence it came - returning to the earth, taking root and waiting to be born again.

This happened within the space of one week, a petal being blown each day....and on the seventh day when the last petal had been taken away on the wind, all that remained of the flower was a withered stem, stripped of all its former beauty.

One of these petals drifted to the top of a high mountain that rose steeply from the eastern side of the garden, where it lodged between two small rocks -and in time, a beautiful Wild Daffodil took root and sprouted.

Another petal blew towards the gushing waters of the nearby stream that flowed down from the mountain, and spilled into a still, silent lake just south of the garden. It landed amidst the wild garlic and blossomed in February. It was born a Snowdrop, and its adopted parents were the early morning mist, and the chill frost of night.

The next petal wafted gently over this lake and into the woods beyond, where it rested amongst the Bluebells and the silky grass that covered the ground beneath the trees - as a carpet covers the floor of a house. This petal blossomed and is known today as a Dandelion.

The fourth petal hovered cautiously in the air, as if deciding itself where it might settle, until eventually it veered over the garden fence towards the foot of the mountain - where it landed in the middle of a vast cornfield which had just recently been ploughed and the fledgling seeds sown. Here the petal lay between the furrows of soil on either side, and here a Rose did eventually bloom.

The next petal to separate from the flower blew westward towards the lush grassland of the Great Orchard, where it weaved between the branches of the large apple trees and floated softly beneath the boughs of the largest tree in the orchard - which happened to be not an apple tree, but a mustard tree. It was the only tree of its kind and was in full bloom. The petal landed safely, and grew to be a perfectly formed Buttercup.

The sixth petal on the little flower awaited the spasmodic gusts of the south westerly wind, and climbed onto its back, heading northwards and was lain down along the roadside which leads to the garden, amidst the wild hawthorn and brambles. It grew to be a member of the widespread Chrysanthemum family, and belonged to the Tansy species.

The seventh and final petal on the flower was tossed high and far into the sky as a gale force wind swept over the garden. It soared northwards and over the roadside, across the open downs towards the steep slopes of the chalk cliffs that looked over the sea. It climbed to the furthermost point until it was very nearly lost forever in the fathomless depths of the raging sea below. But it landed safely on the top of the cliff, clutching tightly to a blade of grass, as the wind howled fiercely like a pied piper to the elements - a magician waving his wand as pebbles, flowers, leaves and insects all plunged over the precipice, helpless and spellbound, like Lemmings' of nature.

The delicate petal clung desperately to the firm blade of grass, and as the wind gradually yawned and fell asleep...a beautiful Orchid took root.

7| The Garden Flowers

Part 2: The Arrival.

I had been meaning to do it for some time......but it had never felt the right time. But that time had now come.

And so I decided to do nothing at all for the space of one week - nothing at all, but to contemplate and to pick flowers. And so I arrived at the garden.

On the first day, I sat in the garden and a gust of wind disturbed my thoughts. I arose and gazed towards the mountain and decided to take a walk.

The next day was calm. I was hot and walked to the waters of the Great Lake for a swim - however, I just sat

sat there and gazed into the still waters. The great wood behind me cast dark reflections and I began to feel cold....it rained heavily that night.

On the following day, it was still raining. The beautiful smells of Nature's baptism found me walking in the rain, and lured to the woods where I took shelter until dusk. A great thunderstorm broke in the night, and I lay awake somewhat perplexed.

Next morning, the rain had ceased and I took the air of the open fields and walked to the nearby cornfield. It was hot.

On the fifth day, the singing of birdsong awoke me very early, and filled me with a sweet yearning for something that seemed forgotten - a memory perhaps; the warm cloak of belonging wrapped tightly around me since childhood. I strolled along to the Orchard and picked apples.

The next day found me in much the same mood, with great sense of nostalgia as I walked along the hedgerows and fields - taking my time. Stopping, listening, bending to peer into the undergrowth. I walked back towards the garden along the road that leads to its north side.

On the seventh and final day of the week, the familiar smell of the sea air was fresh in my nostrils and

I walked to the top of the steep chalk cliffs that overlooked the sea. Here I sat for hours, staring at the horizon with the sea breeze in my face, and the lapping sounds of the sea on the rocks below - like a lullaby gently caressing my yearnings and desires. A solitary fly swept by and disturbed the still waters of my soul, and I returned to the garden.

That evening, after my week of contemplation and walking, I sat very still in the garden - gazing at all the flowers that I had picked on my travels as they radiated a rich array of colour from the little vase of water in which they stood in the middle of the garden. Whilst staring at the flowers, my eyes became heavy and I fell asleep. And in this sleep, I had a dream.....

11 | The Garden Flowers

Part 3: The Dream. The Daffodil's Lament.

A Wild Daffodil is perched high on the topmost peak of a high mountain. It stands alone. The wind swirls furiously all about, and though its petals peel back in sudden gusts revealing its perfect core (like the hair of beautiful woman being combed back, exposing the fullness of her face - unprotected and absolutely pure).....the flower remains unravaged and erect, all at once a monument of praise and a calling for humility within the stark experience of its place within the natural order. He embraces the wind as it passes, and the wind glances back and breathes, "...not yet."

Two climbers watch on from below, aiming to reach the summit. One says to the other, " I wonder what that Marigold is doing up there? I expect he's watching over the land below, and counting how many things he can see, and how far." The other replies, " No, it's not a marigold, but a Yellow Crocus; they often grow up here, so they can assimilate their place in the universe and compare it to others."

They climb on. The route becomes tougher, and the wind grows more fierce. At last, they reach the peak and the first one asks, " Are you a Marigold or a Yellow Crocus?' The Daffodil answers, " I am a flower."

The other asks, " Are you watching over all the land, seeing how many things you can see and how far…or are you wanting to be alone so you can observe everything and therefore assimilate your place in the universe?"

The Daffodil answers, " I am just growing."

Just then, a butterfly glides past and the climbers follow in pursuit, carrying an army of Red Admirals and an allotment of Cabbage Whites on their lips.

The Daffodil sighs and quivers with yearning. He clutches the wind once more, and this time the wind pauses - and then flies like lightning away from the mountain peak.

The Snowdrop's Tears.

A Snowdrop shivers uneasily near the edge of a raging stream. "Why?" he groans...

"Why? Why am I here alone, with only the thunderous roar of this stream calling me to surrender? How my tears have filled the icy waters of this stream and made it the torrent that it is. Will they drown me and bring me to a miserable death? Will they never cease so that I may at last rest for a while, unhappy though I am? How tarnished my leaves and petals have become with the stench of this wild garlic. Everywhere I turn their leaves are turned away from me, and how quickly they are to unravel their own roots from my own. And yet, I can find nowhere to be rid of this smell. A beautiful flower I was born, but no one comes near. Who notices the beauty of a Snowdrop amidst the smell of wild garlic? I watch other flowers on the other side of the stream....how people love to smell their petals, and how joyful their faces look."

The Snowdrop weeps again, and is soothed into a broken sleep by the light rain of evening and the soft caress of moonlight. It hears the faint murmur of the stream whispering..." Come into me, and I will lead you to rest."

The Snowdrop weeps again and tosses its head in an uncontrolled frenzy amidst the sleeping garlic. The

Garlic trembles at the roots and stares in silence at the writhing snowdrop.

"Are you in pain?" it asks, " …can we help you? We know you do not like us, but we have never offended you - we have been afraid of you, for you are a strange flower to us and do not know you."

The Snowdrop's tears begin to pour like a waterfall into the gushing stream - relentless they flow as the stream rages faster and deeper, and begins to tug at the snowdrop's roots. The garlic watches on in fearful anticipation.

All of a sudden, the weeping snowdrop lifts its heavily soaked head and moans with such vigour as to arouse the attention of the sleeping soil beneath. Gently, the soil begins to breathe, as the stream pulls harder at the snowdrop's roots.

In a desperate cry, the Snowdrop screams out, "Forgive me garlic! I must go away from you - forgive me please!"

Then, with tears subsiding and with a feeling of certainty and resolution, the snowdrop gently releases its roots from the firm soil, which in turn, gives way reluctantly - as if sensing an overwhelming feeling of loss and abandonment. The clear flowing waters of the gushing stream sweep the Snowdrop along its course, carrying it between pebbles, rocks and the knarled roots of dead trees lying in the water, until it swells forth into the silent waters of a large, silky pond

- whereupon, the Snowdrop peacefully floats, drifting nowhere in particular….a hypnotic image of tranquility, as silent as the night itself and as urgent as the rolling mist.

The Withered Dandelion.

A Dandelion sits quietly amongst the Foxgloves and Bluebells of a grassy wood. Its flower head has opened and the furry, white pappus awaits patiently for wind dispersal. A young child and his father walk nearby. The child holds a bunch of assorted beautiful flowers in his hand; innocence meeting innocence - nature's most powerful appeal for the heart to melt into charity.

The child plucks a bluebell from the deep grass and notices the Dandelion. "What's that strange looking flower?" He asks his father? 'Oh! It's just a Dandelion" he replies. "There's lots of prettier flowers in the woods than that one. If you blow it, it will just disappear. Here's a pretty Foxglove - see all all its petals like little bells attached to its stem, and smell its beautiful fragrance." The child begins to move forward towards his father but quickly stoops to blow the pollen from the Dandelion's head, whereupon, a mass of fairy-like pollen seeds scatter into the air….rather like birds in flight when the axe strikes the tree. The child watches the pollen seeds float; how they swerve away from objects, how beautifully they drift on the air, how majestic their allusiveness appears. He tries to catch one but misses - he tries again and treads on a Bluebell.

It is time to leave and they disappear out of the wood - the father pointing to Foxgloves, the child looking at his father - watching a Dandelion pollen seed float above his father's head and smiling as another weaves between the stems of the foxgloves to which his father is pointing. All that remains of the Dandelion is a withered stem.

Each day, the child returns to the wood in search of pollen seeds. He finds one and chases it - he loses one, and evening approaches. Before leaving the woods, he goes back to look at the withered stem of the Dandelion. He does not notice the other flowers.

One day, on the way home, he is found contemplating the Dandelion; all the other flowers have been picked by similar small children like himself, with similar fathers'. A pollen seed distracts his attention as it makes its way out of the wood. The child follows, without noticing the absence of the other flowers. All that remains is the withered Dandelion - alone, awaiting the first frost of Autumn.

The Proud Rose.

A crimson Rose stands alone and motionless in the middle of a ploughed cornfield - a breathtaking vision of beauty amidst an isolated land of barreness; a cactus of wonder quenching the thirsty desert of the soul.

The large Oak trees surrounding the fields bow their heads as if in reverence, and the rustle of of the privot hedgerows in the wind could almost be mistaken for the sound of applause in acknowledgement of being witness to nature's manifestation of its Creator.

The Rose watches quietly, an actor taking the final bow on a brightly lit stage, hoping that no cloud will pass over the clear sky above.....that no curtain will bring the show to its close.

" How beautiful I must look," he reflects. "I stand alone, unlike the rest of the other flowers. Their beauty wilts in the dark shade of the Oak trees and they stand together in rows, afraid and all the same. I shall survive when they are dead. I receive the fullness of the sun's light and my beauty abounds alone and unobstructed for all to see.

How pitiful I feel for the corn beneath me, not yet even born - I will survive even the corn. In the harvest, their heads will be threshed and beaten, yet I shall still be here, untouched and undisturbed."

Each day, the Rose dwells on thoughts of this nature, and each day the sunshines brightly and each evening it rains. And the rain washes the Rose clean and fresh for the morning, often leaving several drops on its velvety petals, thus renewing its beauty as all things in nature do when wet - as if their very essence has presented itself in a form of baptismal ritual for the benefit of our souls.

The rain , however, decides not to cease and continues all day and night, and all day again. The Rose is frightened and begins to sway this way and that, swooning with the weight of water inside his flower-head.

The rain beats down even harder.

"Help!" he cries out, "Please help!" But no one hears - he is alone. At the side of the field the other flowers shelter under the mighty boughs of the Oak trees and can only hear the drips of rain on the sodden leaves, and the roar of the babbling stream.

Early next morning, the Rose lies crushed on the ground of the sunlit field, its petals strewn all around. The rain has stopped, as the heads of the corn slowly appear and reach for the sun - having waited patiently under the soil until their time was right.

The Buttercup's Dilemma.

A lone Buttercup flutters gently beneath the branches of a large Mustard tree that stands in the midst of a beautiful Orchard. The Buttercup watches everything in the orchard and stays awake during the night, rather like a sentry on guard; and yet, its beauty never wanes or tires when the early morning light begins to yawn and stretch his thin arms of cloud across the eastern sky.

By day, it watches the other petals arrive in the orchard, and sees them veer clear of the mustard tree and settle beneath the apple and cherry trees - where they grow into all sorts of flowers : Daisies, Primroses and even Buttercups. He sees them make friends with each other and play games with the low hanging apples above. By night, it watches while they slowly close their weary petals and bend softly towards the earth...sometimes resting in groups, often lying across each other; a picture of stillness shrouded by the dark silhouettes of the heavy apples as they cling to the tips of their branches - like a man hanging from the edge of a cliff, knowing the inevitability of not being saved. Dark and heavy apples, pregnant for death, weaving their branches like a web around the sleeping flowers below.

The lone Buttercup watches on - no apples grow on mustard trees, no shroud protects him from the wind and cold; no comfort consoles him in the dead of night.

On the far side of one of the nearby trees, an apple whispers to the buttercup, "Won't you come and join us and share in our games and conversation? Life is too short to be alone - there'll be enough time for that as we apples know only too well! Come, share with us while you can."

The Buttercup flutters uneasily....how nice it would feel to be warm and not lonely anymore; to share laughter and to sleep for a while. Just then, a large bird lands on the branch on which this apple grows, and the apple drops to the ground with a dull thud, slowly rolling past the buttercup and coming to rest against a nearby rock. It lies still and motionless and is badly bruised. The Buttercup trembles a little and observes how separated this apple now looks away from the rest of the apples on the tree...and how none of the flowers beneath even notice. He watches the bird fly away into the distance - and he stays awake all night.

Next morning, he lifts his tired head and sees a man picking apples from the nearby tree and putting them into a basket. The ground below is trodden on, as the Daisies, Primroses and even the other Buttercups all lie crushed and flattened. The man looks at the bruised apple by the rock, pauses, and walks away.

Soon afterwards, the bird returns and makes a nest in the Mustard tree.

By day, the Buttercup watches the bruised apple return to the earth……by night, he listens to the sweet sound of birdsong in the mustard tree.

The Dying Chrysanthemum.

A wild Chrysanthemum, a Tansy, stands amidst a heap of brambles by the side of a dirty road. It faces eastwards.

A large hedgerow separates it from a Poppy field, and the Wild Hawthorn and various assortments of bracken scratch at its petals and knaw at its leafy, angled stems.

A tractor breezes past, as dust and sand fill the air and smother its flower- head. The sudden gust caused by the disturbance rattles the Tansy against the sharp blackberry thorns nearby, and tears its leaves to shreds.

It looks dishevelled and tattered. The dust clears and the Tansy gasps for the fresh wind; but all is calm - there is no wind today.

A little girl, skipping along the road, spies the red shimmer of the Poppies through the green hedgerow but cannot see over the top as she is too small. She tramples on the roadside brambles and peers with some difficulty through the twigs and branches of the hedge. The thorns keep pricking her arms and nettles encircle her vulnerable legs, like crocodiles descending on its prey.

With a squeal, she jumps back into the road and stares very crossly into the overgrowth. Noticing the battered Tansy, she exclaims, "Why aren't you a beautiful flower so I can pick you and put you in a vase? Why haven't you got pretty petals and delicate leaves like those Poppies in the field? I'll never be able to reach them! I wish you weren't so ugly, but then.....you're just a.....just a weed."

Wearily, the Tansy replies, " How do you know what is beautiful until you know what is ugly?"

Puzzled by such an answer, the girl replies somewhat hesitantly, "Well... beautiful is beautiful, like Poppies and Tulips and things. And ugly is ugly - not pretty at all, like spiders and people who die."

"Do you know that I am dying?" answers the Tansy. "No," says the little girl.

"Well I am. Every day at dawn, I look over towards that mountain in the east, for I never sleep now as my cuts and wounds from the thorns give me no rest. The sap pours from my stem daily, and I am growing weaker by the hour.

But each day, I watch the sunrise from behind that mountain and it is very, very beautiful and dear to me.

Sometimes that same sky, only hours later, appears black and thunderous - a very ugly sight to behold, and very fearful also. So what is beautiful and what is ugly? Place a box of spiders beside me as I am now, and am I not beautiful in comparison, torn and battered though I am?" The little girl frowns and tentatively walks away, pauses for a moment, and runs back to brush away a few overhanging brambles above the Tansy. She places some soft, moist grass around the flower to protect it from the wind, and then slowly walks home.

On the next morning at sunrise, the Tansy lies motionless; its flower-head drooping and bowed low - with a tiny trickle of sap on its stem.

The little girl arrives with a vase in her hand and stands over the Tansy, staring without movement, as if in trance.

A field-spider crawls over her shoe, but she doesn't notice.

The Orchid's Obedience.

On the edge of the steep chalk-cliffs facing the sea, a wild Orchid stands - solitary and erect - a phantom of life amidst the raw elements of nature; an intruder into the dancing world of invisible and fundamental forces.

An inquisitive fly hovers and circles around the Orchid, another intruder in awe and fascination of a fellow invader - inspecting, examining, assimilating the new arrival; curious, suspicious, and perhaps somewhat perturbed by the rivalry of territorial claim.

"Hello!", buzzes the fly, as it whizzes past the Orchid's colourful head. The Orchid turns, this way and that to try and reply but cannot see the fly anywhere. All of a sudden, the fly swoops past again and darts to and fro, coming close and then further away, and occasionally hovering somewhat menacingly in front of the Orchid.

"You're a flower aren't you?" The fly asks. "Yes,"replies the Orchid. "Never seen one like you before," retorts the fly, and speeds away - only to

return seconds later on the other side of the flower. The Orchid is puzzled and very confused by the fly's erratic behaviour. "I'm an Orchid", says the Orchid, rather warily. "Orchid!" muses the fly. "Hmm....well it doesn't really matter what you are - you're bound to go the same way as all the rest of them; Pansies, Daisies, Marigolds...all of them. They all end up withered or blown over the cliff, or drowned by the crashing waves of the sea below. They don't last long up here. Sorry to say, but it's a fact....just thought I'd warn you!" Before the Orchid could even think, the fly was gone again - carving a frenzied track into the air, vanishing over the cliff-top, daring to venture near the pounding waves of the sea; and then climbing higher again, almost in playful disregard for the danger of being engulfed by the mighty forces around him.

The Orchid thinks deeply about the fly's discouraging information, and after a while, says determinedly to itself,

" There must always be a flower in this place. I shall remain until the time has come to leave."

In the days that follow, the Orchid experiences the full taste of nature's fruit - torrential rains, thunderstorms, gale force winds, blistering sunshine, and the freezing frosts of night time.

The wind relentlessly pulls at its roots and begs the Orchid to fly away with him. But the Orchid clings desperately to the nearby blades of grass, and often when his strength is waning, the thought of a flower always remaining there on the cliff-top, manages to revive him just enough to hang on for dear life.

The rains pour down heavily without a break, leaving the Orchid gasping for air. Naked and unprotected, it bows his head low beneath its leaves, thinking only of remaining there - and longing to prove that the dismal words of the fly were most definitely premature.

The sunshine constantly beats down with blistering heat, so much so that the poor Orchid's head is reeling drowsily and unable to focus on anything - and he is tempted to lunge over the cliff into the cool waters of the sea, even though sure death would be the outcome. But it remains; with the certainty of night time as consolation and of the setting of the scorching sun.

Thunder and lightning cracks across the mad sky of evening, and the Orchid folds in its petals, so as not to look.

The thunder rumbles through the core of the cliffs and large chunks of rock and chalk splinter and hurtle down the precipice and into the looming mouth of the sea below. The Orchid, trembling without restraint, stands crying and weeping on the point of despair.

For how long the Orchid remained weeping, with almost heroic dignity and integrity no one knows.

The storm has now ceased, and it is early morning. A thick fog has enveloped the cliff-top and the Orchid knows it has lost its battle. His strength and his fight have all gone. He awaits the first strong wind to surrender to but finds there is no wind today. The fog has ice riding on its wings, and the Orchid is filled with a numb sense of nothingness and detachment.

A sudden sea breeze pulls the curtains of cloud back from the sun's face and blows the fog gently away.

As it does so, the Orchid wrenches itself from the moist, chalky earth and climbs onto its wing, floating high into the air.

It glances back at the spot where it had been growing all this time, and through the clearing mist, notices a tiny

petal - right next to where it had been, which the storm must have blown there during the night. The Orchid releases itself from the fingers of the wind, and floats slowly down to the cliff-top, landing beside the new little petal. The petal turns and grips tightly to the Orchid's roots as the wind begins to sneeze.

29| The Garden Flowers

Part 4: The Departure

I awoke suddenly. In front of me stood a vase of water in the middle of the garden - in which seven withered stems drooped and leaned over. I dug a shallow hole in the centre of the garden lawn and placed the seven stems within it, burying them with the surrounding soil.

I paused, and knew with some certainty and conviction, that I would be standing in that same garden again in exactly one year's time....and for every year to follow as long as my life continues.

I opened the gate and walked pensively along the dusty road, and took one last glance back at the garden.

I walked away.

As I looked up towards the mountain, I thought for a moment that I spotted on the topmost mountain peak, a thin, solitary silhouette against the bright sky. A pollen seed distracted my attention......and I walked on.

www.ingramcontent.com/pod-product-compliance
Lightning Source LLC
Chambersburg PA
CBHW050027170726
48282CB00025B/574
* 9 7 8 9 3 7 3 1 0 7 4 3 1 *